JASON STRANGE

Text 4 REVENGE

Illustrated by Alberto Dal Lago

STONE ARCH BOOKS
a capstone imprint

Jason Strange is published by
Stone Arch Books
A Capstone Imprint
151 Good Counsel Drive, P.O. Box 669
Mankato, Minnesota 56002
www.capstonepub.com

Library of Congress Cataloging-in-Publication Data is available at the Library of
Congress website.

Summary: Thirteen-year-old Adam died in a skateboard accident three days ago--so
why are his best friends still getting text messages from him?

978-1-4342-3233-5 (library binding)
978-1-4342-3432-2 (pbk.)

Art Director/Graphic Designer: Kay Fraser
Production Specialist: Michelle Biedscheid

Photo credits:
Shutterstock: Nikita Rogul (handcuffs, p. 2); Stephen Mulcahey (police badge, p. 2);
B&T Media Group (blank badge, p. 2); Picsfive (coffee stain, pp. 2, 5, 12, 17, 24, 30,
42, 48, 57); Andy Dean Photography (paper, pen, coffee, pp. 2, 66); osov (blank notes,
p. 1); Thomas M Perkins (folder with blank paper, pp. 66, 67); M.E. Mulder (black
electrical tape, pp. 5, 10, 17, 23, 31, 38, 41, 48, 53, 59, 69, 70, 71)

Printed in the United States of America in Stevens Point, Wisconsin.
032011
006111WZF11

TABLE OF CONTENTS

— Chapter 1: The First Message —

It was a sunny day. But to James, Kurt, and Garrett, it felt like the cloudiest day ever.

"I still can't believe it," James said. He was sitting on the grass, his skateboard resting next to him.

Kurt shook his head. "Me either," he said. He sat down on the curb.

"This time last week, all four of us were skating around Dimlight Park," Garrett said. He pushed his skateboard back and forth.

"Would you quit that?" Kurt finally said. "You're driving me crazy."

"Yeah," James said. "It's pretty annoying." He spun the wheels on his board.

Garrett jumped down from his board. "Jeez, sorry," he said.

"You too, James," Kurt said. "Cut it out."

"Boy, you're sure whining a lot today," James said. He gave the wheel an extra hard spin. It whirred loudly.

"That's it," Kurt said. He grabbed the board from James's chest.

"Hey!" James said, sitting up.

"You want it back?" Kurt said. He stood up and threw it with all his might into the woods. "Go get it, then."

James jumped up and dove at Kurt.

The two boys rolled on the grass, each struggling to get on top. Garrett hurried over and pulled at James's arms. "Hey, break it up!" Garrett said. "Quit it, you guys."

Finally, Kurt rolled James onto his back and sat down on his stomach.

"Get off," James said.

"Make me," Kurt said, narrowing his eyes.

Garrett grabbed James's shirt and pulled him off. "I'll make you," he said. "Both of you, stop being morons."

"Shut up," James said. "He started it."

Kurt laughed. "Yeah, right," he muttered. "You're the one being annoying."

"And you're the one acting like a baby," James said.

"You're both being babies," Garrett said.

"I'm going to get my board," James said. He stomped off toward the woods.

A sedan came slowly up Mountain Drive. "There's my mom," Garrett said. "Are you two going to be okay?"

"Yeah," Kurt said. "I just got mad. But I'll be fine. It won't happen again."

Garrett nodded. "I know," he said. "I'm mad too." Garrett looked over Kurt's shoulder. "See you later, James!" he called.

The car pulled up to the curb and Garrett opened the passenger door. He got in.

Garrett's mom asked, "Is everything okay? Kurt looked upset."

"He's fine," Garrett said. "Or he's not. I don't know. Do you know what I mean?"

"I think so," she said.

Garrett looked out the window as they drove back down the hill toward their house in downtown Ravens Pass.

"Ever since Adam died three days ago, we've all felt so angry," Garrett said. "We just miss him."

His mom took his hand, and he didn't pull it away. "I know," she said.

Garrett felt a vibration in his pocket and reached for his phone. "Text message. It's probably Kurt, texting me to tell me how annoying James is," he said.

He looked at the caller ID: New message from ADAM.

Garrett quickly flipped open his phone and read the note.

Don't let them bury me.

— Chapter 2: Get Him —

Dinner seemed to last forever. Garrett ate quickly, but his parents wouldn't let him leave the table until they were done eating too.

They ate slowly. They talked about boring things. Garrett tapped his foot anxiously under the table.

"Are you in a hurry, Gar?" his dad asked.

"I'm supposed to meet Kurt and James at the school," he said.

He hadn't shown his mom the text message. It was too creepy. But he had to talk it over with his friends. Before dinner, he'd sent a quick note to them both telling them to meet him at the old jungle gym.

"And it's a matter of national importance?" Garrett's father joked.

Garrett sighed.

"Go ahead," his father said after a moment. "Have a good time."

Garrett jumped up. "Thanks," he said. Then he grabbed his board from the front closet and headed out the door.

* * *

The sun was almost down by the time Garrett rolled up to the playground behind the elementary school.

Garrett, James, and Kurt were in eighth grade. Still, they liked to hang out at the elementary school jungle gym if they didn't feel like seeing anyone else.

Adam had been in eighth grade too. Then he had taken a bad fall on his board at the biggest skate park in Ravens Pass, Clyde's Skate Park.

Garrett hadn't been there that morning. It was too early. But Adam was very serious about skating. He often got up at dawn, even on weekends, to practice.

James was sitting on a swing when Garrett got to the elementary school playground.

Kurt was hanging from the monkey bars. "Hey, Gar," he called out. Then he jumped down. "Crazy, huh?"

"You guys too?" Garrett asked. "Same message?"

James nodded. "We both got it. 'Don't bury me,'" he said. "Creepy."

"Very," Garrett said. He got chills as he remembered seeing Adam's name on the caller ID.

Kurt walked over to Garrett. "So I have one question," Kurt said. "Who do we know with a sense of humor that's sick enough to send a message like that?"

James wrapped his arms around the swing's chains. "And who has Adam's cell phone?"

"His brother," Kurt said. "It can't be anyone else."

Garrett looked at his sneakers and fiddled with his board.

"I don't know," Garrett said. "Scott was so depressed. He's really sad about Adam."

Kurt kicked the sand under the swing set. "Yeah," he said. "That's true. I doubt he'd want to joke around right now."

Garrett shook his head. "No way."

Kurt sat on the second step of the play set. He snapped his fingers and said, "Paul Tontino."

Garrett thought it over. Paul had given him and his friends — including Adam — a hard time for years. He called them freaks and weirdos on a regular basis. He was also two years older than them and still in eighth grade. He was the only kid in middle school with a car.

James jumped off his swing. "Definitely," he said. "Let's go find him."

"Now you're talking," Kurt said. He punched his left palm with his right fist.

"No way, you guys," Garrett said. "He'll flatten us."

"Not all three of us at once," Kurt said. "Let's get him. For Adam."

Garrett took a deep breath. "How could it be him?" he asked. "Paul doesn't have Adam's phone."

Kurt shrugged. "Maybe he beat up Scott and stole it," he said.

"Yeah," Garrett said. "He'd do it."

The three of them stood in a little triangle, each of them holding his skateboard.

"All right," Garrett said. "Let's go."

– Chapter 3: Help Me –

It was dark by the time they reached Paul's house on Freshkill Lake. It was a big house. Paul's familiar sports car, bright orange with red and yellow flames along the sides, was in the driveway.

The boys skated right up the driveway. They stopped in front of the big double doors.

Garrett and James glanced at each other. Kurt rolled his eyes.

"It's just a doorbell, guys," Kurt said. Then he reached out and pressed the button. The bell was loud and musical, like a big church organ was being played.

"Yeah?" a voice said. It sounded like it was probably Paul's father. "Who is it? What are you selling?"

"Um," Kurt said. "We, uh . . ."

"Is Paul home, sir?" Garrett asked quickly.

"You friends of his?" the voice said through the door.

"We know him from school," Garrett replied. He didn't want to say they were Paul's friends, since they definitely were not.

The voice didn't reply. After a few seconds, James spoke up. "I guess he decided not to let us in," he said. "Let's go."

"Wait a second," Garrett said. He heard footsteps from the other side of the door. Then it swung open. Paul Tontino stood there in baggy shorts and a white tank top. He was holding a wireless game controller.

When he saw the three boys on his stoop, he smiled a wicked smile. "What do you morons want?" he asked.

Kurt swallowed. "Paul," he said. "We . . ."

"What?" Paul said. "Spit it out, dweeb."

"You heard about Adam?" Garrett asked.

Paul bit his lip and looked down. "Yeah," he said quietly. "I'm sorry."

"What are you sorry about?" James asked.

Paul shrugged. "That's what you say," he said. "You know, when someone dies. It's really dumb that he died, that's all."

"Yeah, it does," Garrett said. "Look, we gotta go. Sorry to bug you." He grabbed James and Kurt by the collars and pulled them away from the door.

When the door had closed, Garrett got on his board and pushed off toward the road. His friends followed.

"He didn't do it," Garrett said. "He's a bully. But he's not a psychopath."

"So now what?" Kurt asked. He passed Garrett, hit the street, and headed fast back toward the center of town. James and Garrett sped along to keep up.

"I guess we can forget about it," Garrett said. "Unless you have another idea."

Just then Garrett felt his phone vibrate. "Hold up," he called to his friends, but he didn't need to bother.

They'd both stopped already and were reaching for their own cell phones.

The three boys looked at each other.

"Another one," James said.

They all opened their phones. Garrett looked at his screen. It was from Adam again.

It's me, for real. Don't forget this. Help me.

Garrett felt the blood leave his face.

"Now what?" James said.

Garrett looked at the sky. The moon was full and bright. "I think we should do what he says," he said quietly.

"Who?" James asked. "The moon?"

Garrett shook his head. "No," he said. "Adam."

– Chapter 4: Adam's Skateboard –

The next morning, the boys knocked on the door of the Weir and Sons funeral home. It was the only funeral home in town, right on the edge of the cemetery.

The funeral director, Mr. Weir, opened the door. He was a short man with a bushy mustache. He had thick glasses that made his eyes look big and buggy.

"Hi, Mr. Weir," James said. "We're friends of Adam Quinn's."

Mr. Weir blinked. "Oh yes," he said. "The skateboarder." He opened the door wider and held out his arm to the room behind him. "Come in."

"Thanks," James said. The three boys went inside.

"Sit, sit," Mr. Weir said. He sat down in a chair. The boys sat together on the couch.

"How can I help you?" Mr. Weir asked.

"This is going to sound kind of crazy," Garrett said.

"That's an understatement," Kurt muttered.

"I'm sorry, you'll have to speak up," Mr. Weir said. He leaned forward in his chair.

Garrett glared at Kurt. Then he said, louder, "The thing is, we've been getting these text messages."

"From Adam," James put in.

"Adam?" Mr. Weir said. "The deceased?"

"Right," Garrett said. Now he glared at James. "I was getting to that."

"I'm afraid I don't understand," Mr. Weir said.

"I'm not sure we do either," Garrett said. This was harder than he thought it would be. "But the thing is, all three of us got the same two messages from Adam — or from his phone, anyway."

"Well," Mr. Weir said. He pushed his glasses up his nose. "There are two strange things about that."

"Just two?" Kurt muttered.

"One: Adam's phone was left with his parents," Mr. Weir went on. "And two: your friend is, I'm sorry to say, passed."

"But are you sure?" Garrett asked.

Mr. Weir sat up straight. "Young man," he said. "I have been a funeral director since I was nineteen years old. I promise you, I know a dead person when I see one."

"Can we . . . ," Garrett began, stammering. "Can we see him?"

Mr. Weir squinted at the boys. "Is this some kind of high school prank?" he asked.

"We're not in high school," James said. "Just eighth grade."

Garrett shushed him. "It's not a joke, Mr. Weir," he said. "Honest. We're just worried about our friend. It feels terrible to get text messages like this. You can see our phones."

All three boys dug into their pockets and pulled out their phones. They held them out toward Mr. Weir.

The funeral director pulled off his glasses and took a handkerchief from his chest pocket. As he polished the lenses, he shook his head slowly.

"Adam's viewing is later today," Mr. Weir finally said. He slipped his glasses back on. "The body is prepared already. I don't think it would do any harm to let his three best friends have an early look." He stood up. "Follow me."

The three boys jumped to their feet. They followed Mr. Weir through a swinging door. He headed down a hallway to a quiet, dark room.

Mr. Weir stopped beside a table. There was a coffin on top. Lying inside, in a black suit, was Adam. His skateboard was propped up against the table.

"Oh," James said. "Adam."

"There you have it," Mr. Weir said. "Would you like me to leave you boys for a moment?"

"No," Garrett said quickly. "Why is his skateboard here?"

"I always offer to have something buried with the deceased," Mr. Weir said. "Adam's parents said his skateboard was his favorite thing in the world."

James nodded. "They're right," he said. "He would have wanted it with him."

Garret turned and headed for the stairs. "We're sorry to have bothered you," he said.

"It's no bother," Mr. Weir said. "But it seems that someone is playing a joke on you three. And not a very funny one."

Kurt stared at his friend lying on the table. He shook his head and said quietly, "No, not funny at all."

* * *

Outside, the three boys walked, carrying their boards. When they were far enough from the cemetery, Kurt sat on a bench at a bus stop. "That was not what I expected," he said.

The other boys nodded. Then Garrett felt his pocket buzz. "Another message," he said.

"You read it," James said. "I don't want to."

"Me either," Kurt said.

Garrett flipped open his phone and read the message.

It's no joke. And you're not crazy.

– Chapter 5: Go –

"I don't think we should do this, guys,"
Garrett said.

He, James, and Kurt were standing
in the street in front of Adam's family's
house. They'd been standing there for a few
minutes, while Kurt and James tried to be
brave enough to ring the bell.

"Garrett, we went along with you to the
funeral home," Kurt said. "And now he
thinks we're a bunch of bananas."

James nodded. "Now it's time to check with Adam's family," he said. "Just go along with it."

Garrett shrugged. "Okay," he said. "If you guys say so. But I'm not standing in the street like an idiot anymore. I'm going to ring the bell."

He strolled across the lawn toward the door and rang the bell.

Adam's mom opened the door. She seemed sad, but her face brightened when she saw the boys. "James, Kurt, Garrett," she said. She stepped back. "Come in, please."

"Good morning, Ms. Quinn," Kurt said.

"You boys have a seat in the TV room," she said. "I'll get you a few sodas, okay?"

"Oh, that's okay. We just wanted to tell you about these —" James started to say.

Garrett cut him off. "Thanks, Ms. Quinn," he said. "We'd love some sodas." He nudged James and Kurt and started heading for the TV room.

"Just sit down," Garrett hissed at his friends. "We have to be careful. She's probably barely keeping it together. We can't just burst out about the text messages."

"Okay, okay," James said.

Ms. Quinn appeared with three cans of soda. She put them on the coffee table. Kurt grabbed one and popped it open quickly.

Ms. Quinn sat down in the big chair next to the couch. "How have you boys been?" she asked. "I'm sorry we haven't had a chance to talk since Adam's accident."

"We've been okay," James said. "I mean, pretty sad."

Ms. Quinn nodded. "So have we," she said quietly.

Kurt took a deep breath and put down his soda. Then he leaned forward. "We actually came to show you something," he said. "Or to ask you something. Do you have Adam's phone?"

Ms. Quinn seemed surprised by the question. "I suppose so," she said. "Is there some reason you need it?"

"We just want to see it," Garrett said. "We'll explain."

"I'll go and grab it," she said. "Then you can tell me what this is all about."

When she came back, she handed Garrett the phone. He flipped it open and clicked a couple of buttons to get to the text message SENT folder.

"Anything?" James said. He leaned over to get a peek at the screen.

Garrett shook his head. "Nope," he said. "Nothing sent since that morning."

Ms. Quinn crossed her arms. "What is going on, boys?" she asked.

"We've been getting these text messages," James said. He took out his phone and opened it to show Ms. Quinn. "They say they're from Adam."

Ms. Quinn's face went pale and she opened her mouth, but didn't speak. She just put one hand over her mouth and with the other took James's phone.

Her eyes darted across the words on the screen. Her thumb clicked to the next message. She closed her mouth, and her eyes filled with tears.

"What is this?" she whispered. Her eyes finally left the screen and she looked from one boy to the next.

Adam's dad came in just then. "Hello, boys," he said. Then he noticed his wife's tears. "What's wrong?"

He put an arm around his wife and took James's phone from her. He looked at the messages. "What is this?" he asked. "Is this supposed to be funny?"

"No, Mr. Quinn," Kurt said. "We—"

"Just go, please," Mr. Quinn said. Ms. Quinn now stood with her face in her hands. She was sobbing.

"We didn't mean to upset anyone," Garrett said.

"Well, you have," Mr. Quinn said. He pointed toward the front door. "Go."

Chapter 6: More Messages

Before long, the boys were back at the elementary school, hanging around the old jungle gym.

"That's the last time I listen to you two," Garrett said. He sat on the edge of the play area and slid his board back and forth.

"How could we know that Adam's mom would react like that?" Kurt asked.

Garrett frowned. "I knew," he said.

"Oh yeah?" Kurt said. "You're so much smarter than us, huh? How smart will you be with my skateboard in your mouth?"

Just then, the boys' phones all vibrated at once. James grabbed his phone and read the new text message.

Stop fighting, you idiots.

"We can't ignore this," Garrett said. "Adam is trying to contact us."

"But why?" Kurt said. "Why would he want us to stop the funeral? He's dead, isn't he? We saw him."

Garrett sat down at the end of the slide. "In a lot of stories," he said, "ghosts who contact friends need help solving a murder."

"Adam wasn't murdered," Kurt said. "He took a really bad spill on his board."

"Maybe it's not that simple," Garrett said. "Maybe someone's responsible. Maybe once Adam is buried, we won't be able to prove it."

"So there's evidence in his pocket or something?" Kurt asked.

"Adam's board," James said. "He's being buried with his skateboard."

"That's it!" Garrett said. "The board will prove it was not an accident."

"Let's go, then," Kurt said. "The viewing is going on right now. Let's go get the board."

"We can't just walk in and take the board," Garrett said. "We'll have to break in tonight and check it out."

"Break in?" James repeated. "Are you serious?"

Garrett nodded. "Very serious," he said.

— Chapter 7: Breaking and Entering —

"This is stupid," Kurt said. "Scratch that. This is insane."

"And illegal," James said.

The rear entrance to the funeral home was only twenty yards away. They'd already watched the security guard lock the door and start his rounds of the cemetery.

"We haven't broken any laws yet," Garrett said. "You can run home and watch cartoons."

"I'm here, aren't I?" James said.

"Okay then," Garrett said. "We're here to help Adam, and his family. If Mr. and Ms. Quinn are going to forgive us for what happened this morning, this is a good start."

"Breaking in and stealing his skateboard will make them forgive us?" Kurt asked. "I doubt it."

"It will if it proves who is responsible for his accident," Garrett said. "Now shush, here comes the guard again."

The guard came around from the front of the funeral home. He was a carrying a long metal flashlight.

"That round took about fifteen minutes," Garrett said. "That means we won't have long to get in and out before he comes around again."

"We are going to get arrested," James muttered. "I'll never finish middle school."

"Are you ready?" Garrett asked. As soon as the guard was out of sight, he jogged toward the back door. James and Kurt stayed close behind him.

"So how do we get in, genius?" Kurt said.

Garrett looked around, then headed for the porch on the side. Kurt and James followed.

There was a big window into the building from the porch. Garrett forced it open. Then he started to climb in.

"This is crazy," James muttered. But he and Kurt followed their friend inside.

With the lights off, the funeral home was extra creepy. They'd climbed right into the viewing room.

At the front of the room was a huge display of flowers. Garrett squinted into the dark and didn't see a coffin.

"Are we too late?" Kurt whispered. "Adam's coffin is gone."

"Maybe Mr. Weir brought Adam back downstairs," Garrett said. He headed for the swinging door in the back.

The boys took the stairs down to a cold room. The metal table in the middle of the room was empty. Along the wall, several small metal doors were closed.

"Maybe inside one of those doors," Kurt suggested.

James shivered. "Isn't that where they keep the bodies?" he asked.

"I guess we have to check," Garrett said. "And quick. That guard will be back soon."

Kurt ran over to the refrigerator doors and started throwing them open. Soon all ten doors were wide open. The boys went from door to door. Three were empty, but the others weren't. But Adam wasn't inside.

"Now what do we do?" James asked.

Kurt shrugged. He said, "We're about to get busted for breaking and entering."

"Keep your voices down," Garrett hissed. He looked around, hoping for an idea. "If that guard passes the house, I don't want to be heard. Adam must be upstairs. Come on."

Garrett led the way back upstairs. He pushed open the swinging door and spotted a flashlight beam on the far wall. He let the door swing closed and pushed his friends backward. "There's someone in there," he whispered. "We have to hide."

The boys quickly found a closet and dove inside, leaving the door open a crack.

"The guard must have heard us moving around," James said. "We are so busted."

"Shh," Kurt said. "Just stay quiet."

Peeking through the open closet door, Garrett saw the flashlight beam dancing on the wall. "Here he comes," he whispered.

Just then, the boys' phones vibrated.

"Oh, not now, Adam," Kurt whispered. He grabbed his phone and held the screen up to his face. "Guys. Look."

He held out the phone. The glow of his screen fell over Garrett's face as he read the short message.

Not the guard. Hurry!

Chapter 8: Inside

Garrett pulled the closet door closed.

The footsteps outside were slow and heavy. Whoever it was didn't seem to worry about getting caught in the funeral home.

"Who could it be?" James whispered. Garrett elbowed him to shut him up.

Soon the footsteps stopped outside the closet. Garret gasped and closed his eyes. None of the boys breathed.

The doorknob jiggled. The boys leaned against the closet's back wall.

"Hello?" a voice called from the other room. The doorknob stopped jiggling, and the boys heard footsteps thumping down the stairs. Soon another set of footsteps, running, followed down the steps.

"The real guard must have found whoever it is," James said. "Now's our chance to get out of here."

"We'll run right into the guard," Kurt said.

"We have to risk it," Garrett said. "Let's go." He threw open the door and went right for the swinging door to the front room. "There," he said, pointing at the wall. There was a line of coffins he hadn't noticed before.

Kurt opened the first one. "I found him," he said.

The boys stood around the coffin. There was Adam, in his suit, with his skateboard across his chest.

Just then, all of their phones vibrated.

He's coming. Grab it and run.

"Grab what?" James asked.

Garrett nodded. "The board." He carefully slid it away. He closed the lid of the coffin. Then he ran to the window. It was locked.

"The guard must have locked it," Garrett said. "We'll have to try the door."

Suddenly, the swinging door flew open. A man stomped into the room. He looked like he'd been in a fight.

"What did you do to the guard?" Garrett asked. He held the skateboard behind his back.

The man waved him off. He walked right to Adam's coffin and opened it.

"Hey, leave him alone," Kurt shouted. "That's our friend."

The man closed the lid and turned to face the boys. "Is that right?" he said. "Then you skate rats probably know why I'm here."

Garrett gripped the board behind his back even tighter. Meanwhile, James worked on the back door. It seemed to have about ten different locks.

"So, which of you has his skateboard?" the man asked.

"Come on, James," Garrett muttered. "Open that door!"

"Got it!" James shouted. The door flew open and the boys sprinted out into the cemetery.

"He's gaining on us," James yelled as they ran. "Man, he sure doesn't look that fast."

"In there," Garrett said. He pointed at a small stone building in the center of the graveyard.

"The mausoleum?" Kurt asked. "Can this night get any creepier?"

"We don't have a choice," Garrett said. He pulled open the heavy metal door and went in.

Once Kurt and James were inside too, he pushed the door closed. The boys ran to the back of the square room and hid behind a stone tomb.

"I think it's time to get some help," Kurt said quietly. He opened his phone. "I'm calling the cops."

Garrett nodded. "Okay," he said. "We already have what we came for." He held up the skateboard.

Kurt punched some buttons on his phone.

"Who is that guy, anyway?" James asked. "What does he want with Adam's board?"

"Uh-oh," Kurt said. "No cell service in here."

"I'm not surprised," Garrett said. "We're in a cell with thick concrete walls."

Then Kurt's phone began to vibrate. The boys froze.

"I guess the signal is strong enough for Adam to get through," James muttered.

Kurt opened the phone and read the message out loud.

`He's right outside the door. Use the back way.`

Garrett looked over his shoulder. A small metal grate near the floor was the only possible way out. "We'll have to squeeze through," he said.

James got down on his knees and lifted the grate away. He barely fit. Once he was through, Kurt followed. The two boys helped Garrett push through too.

Another message came through from Adam.

Run toward the light. He's coming.

Garrett spun, looking for a light in the darkness. Between the old hanging maple trees, he spotted an iron lamppost. "That way," he said. He started running.

"Stop!" a booming voice called out.

Kurt and James ran after Garrett. "We'll never get away," James said. "Even if we reach the light."

"Just don't stop," Garrett said. "Adam wouldn't steer us wrong."

The boys dodged between thick, knotted tree trunks, barely turning in time in the shadowy half light.

Garrett stopped short. A fence was in his way.

"Dead end," Kurt said. "So much for Adam's help."

"There!" James shouted. Past the fence, less than half a block away, a police car was parked under the street lamp.

"We can't get to it," Garrett said. "The only way out is behind us, next to the funeral home."

"Scream," James said. "Scream!"

"Hey, officer!" Garrett yelled. "Help us!"

"Help!" Kurt joined in. Soon all three boys were hollering at the top of their lungs.

"Got you," the big man said. He stepped right to them and grabbed Garrett's collar. "Give me that board. Without it, no one can prove my company is at fault for that boy's death."

"What's going on over here?" the policeman asked, walking up to the fence. "Take your hands off that boy."

– Chapter 10: Bad for Business –

"You boys, don't move," the officer said. He was handcuffing the big man. "After we take care of this guy," the officer went on, "we're going to need to ask you some questions."

"Okay," Garrett said.

"Now let's get a look at this board," James said. He took the board from Garrett. After looking at it for a second, he said, "Huh."

"What is it?" Kurt asked.

"These are new trucks," James said. "And there's a wicked crack right here."

"It wasn't my fault," the big man said. He hung his head, finally giving up. "We got a bad shipment of trucks down at the park store."

"You're Clyde," Garrett said. "The park owner."

The man nodded. "I knew they were faulty, but we needed money," he said. "Your friend bought the first one out of the box."

"And then he crashed," James said.

"We stopped selling them right away," Clyde said, looking at the police officer. "But if it got out that your friend had been using one of those trucks, I would have lost everything. The accident was bad enough for business."

"So you had to steal the board from his coffin," Garrett said.

"I knew if I didn't, one of his friends would see it," Clyde said. "And I was right."

Kurt patted Clyde on the shoulder. "Actually, you weren't," he said. "Adam told us about it."

Clyde stared at Kurt, then at Garrett and James. "What do you mean?" he asked. "You must have seen the board at the viewing."

"We weren't even at the viewing," James said. He pulled out his phone just as it began to vibrate. "That's him now."

James opened the phone and held it up to Clyde to read the message.

"What's it say?" James asked. "Read it to us."

"It says, 'Thanks, guys. Now leave him to me,'" Clyde read. "Is this a joke?" he asked, looking up.

Garrett shook his head. "No joke," he said. The wind picked up. The branches around them began to tremble and shake. Suddenly, the funeral home's back door flew open.

The wind whooshed in their ears. Clyde's thin hair flew back in the face of the strong breeze.

"You guys, I think Adam's coming," Kurt said.

Garrett nodded. "Let's head over to the front gate and find that cop," he said. "I'm sure Adam can handle this guy."

The boys walked off, leaving Clyde trembling against the iron fence.

As they left, Garrett took once last glance over his shoulder. He saw Clyde's mouth open in fear as an inky shadow slid across the cemetery ground, dodging between trees like a skateboard, and headed right for him.

Case number: 786544

Date reported: August 14

Crime scene: Weir & Sons Funeral Home, Ravens Pass

Local police: Officer Charles Petersen, with the force 25 years

Civilian witnesses: Garrett Wilson, age 13; James Gregors, age 13; Kurt Byron, age 13; Clyde Harbinger, age 37, owner of Clyde's Skate Park; Jebadiah Townsend, age 89, Weir & Sons night security guard

Disturbance: Attack by supernatural force. Victim (Harbinger) is in stable condition at Ravens Pass General Hospital.

Suspect information: None, though some of the witnesses believe it was their recently deceased friend, Adam Quinn.

CASE NOTES:

I WAS CALLED IN JUST AFTER MIDNIGHT. OFFICER
PETERSEN, AS WELL AS THREE EMTs FROM RPGH,
WERE ON THE SCENE. HARBINGER WAS IN SHOCK,
BUT THE THREE TEENAGERS FILLED ME IN ON WHAT
HAD HAPPENED. APPARENTLY, HARBINGER HAD JUST
ADMITTED TO TRYING TO COVER UP THE FACT THAT
HIS FAULTY EQUIPMENT HAD CAUSED THE DEATH OF
ADAM QUINN, AGE 13, A FEW DAYS AGO. THE FRIENDS
CAME ACROSS HARBINGER TAMPERING WITH THE ONLY
EVIDENCE THAT COULD PROVE HIS INVOLVEMENT. HE
TRIED TO CHASE THEM, BUT OFFICER PETERSEN WAS
NEARBY.

OFFICER PETERSEN SAID HE WALKED AWAY TO CALL
FOR BACKUP AND HEARD SCREAMS. HE THOUGHT THE
BOYS HAD ATTACKED HARBINGER, BUT HARBINGER SAID
IT WAS SOME KIND OF SHADOW.

HARBINGER HAS BEEN ARRESTED. HE'LL FACE TRIAL
IN A COUPLE OF MONTHS. IN THE MEANTIME, CLYDE'S
SKATE PARK WILL BE RUN BY VOLUNTEERS. I DON'T
EXPECT ANY FURTHER DISTURBANCES.

DEAR READER,

THEY ASKED ME TO WRITE ABOUT MYSELF. THE FIRST
THING YOU NEED TO KNOW IS THAT JASON STRANGE IS
NOT MY REAL NAME. IT'S A NAME I'VE TAKEN TO HIDE MY
TRUE IDENTITY AND PROTECT THE PEOPLE I CARE ABOUT.
YOU WOULDN'T BELIEVE THE THINGS I'VE SEEN, WHAT I'VE
WITNESSED. IF PEOPLE KNEW I WAS TELLING THESE STORIES,
SHARING THEM WITH THE WORLD, THEY'D TRY TO GET ME TO
STOP. BUT THESE STORIES NEED TO BE TOLD, AND I'M THE
ONLY ONE WHO CAN TELL THEM.

I CAN'T TELL YOU MANY DETAILS ABOUT MY LIFE. I CAN TELL
YOU I WAS BORN IN A SMALL TOWN AND LIVE IN ONE STILL. I
CAN TELL YOU I WAS A POLICE DETECTIVE HERE FOR TWENTY-
FIVE YEARS BEFORE I RETIRED. I CAN TELL YOU I'M STILL
OUT THERE EVERY DAY AND THAT CRAZY THINGS ARE STILL
HAPPENING.
I'LL LEAVE YOU WITH ONE QUESTION—IS ANY OF THIS TRUE?

JASON STRANGE
RAVENS PASS

Glossary

deceased (di-SEEST)—a person who is dead

depressed (di-PREST)—feeling sad or gloomy

dodge (DOJ)—moving quickly from side to side

familiar (fuh-MIL-yur)—known or recognized

mausoleum (maw-suh-LEE-uhm)—a large building that houses a tomb or tombs

psychopath (SYE-kuh-path)—someone who is violent and dangerous

responsible (ri-SPON-suh-buhl)—the cause or fault of something

round (ROUND)—a regular route

trucks (TRUHKS)—the axle units on skateboards to which the wheels are attached

understatement (UHN-dur-stayt-muhnt)—saying that something is less than it is

vibrate (VYE-brate)—to shake or move back and forth rapidly

DISCUSSION QUESTIONS

1. Why did Adam send the text messages?

2. If you could be one of the characters in this book, who would you want to be? Explain your answer.

3. What are some healthy ways to grieve when someone dies?

WRITING PROMPTS

1. Has someone close to you died? Write about how you feel about that person.

2. Imagine this story from Adam's point of view. Try writing the last chapter from his perspective.

3. In this book, the four boys were best friends. Write about your best friends. Who are they? What are they like? What do you do together?